Amina's Blanket

Crabtree Publishing Company
www.crabtreebooks.com

PMB 16A, 350 Fifth Avenue
Suite 3308
New York, NY 10118

612 Welland Avenue
St. Catharines, Ontario
Canada, L2M 5V6

Dunmore, Helen, 1952-
    Amina's blanket / Helen Dunmore ; illustrated by Paul Dainton.
        p. cm. -- (Yellow bananas)
        Summary: After helping to knit and sew together the squares of a blanket to
be sent to a country at war, Josie dreams of what life is like for the girl who will
receive the blanket as a gift from Josie's class.
        ISBN 0-7787-0938-8 (RHC.) -- ISBN 0-7787-0984-1
(pbk.)
        [1. Blankets--Fiction. 2. War--Fiction. 3. Dreams--Fiction. 4.
Schools--Fiction.] I. Dainton, Paul, ill. II. Title. III. Series.
PZ7.D92147 Am 2003
[Fic]--dc21
                                    2002009609
                                    LC

Published by Crabtree Publishing in 2002
Published in 2000 by Egmont Children's Books Limited
Text copyright © Helen Dunmore 1996
Illustrations copyright © Paul Dainton 2000
The Author and Illustrator have asserted their moral rights.
Reinforced Hardcover Binding ISBN 0-7787-0938-8 Paperback ISBN 0-7787-0984-1

1 2 3 4 5 6 7 8 9 0 Printed in Italy 0 9 8 7 6 5 4 3 2

Amina's Blanket

Helen Dunmore

Illustrated by Paul Dainton

YELLOW BANANAS

For my parents
P.D.

Chapter One

"JOSIE!" MISS HEATHER'S voice cracked across the classroom. Josie jumped.

"Dreaming again!" scolded Miss Heather. "Well, you nearly missed something very exciting."

But Josie couldn't believe that anything exciting was going to happen at ten o'clock on a wet Monday morning in Miss Heather's class.

"Okay!" said Miss Heather. "Wait two minutes and I'll bring it in."

Then she went out with a mysterious smile, leaving the door open. What was she talking about? Josie stared across the table at Natasha.

5

"Blankets!" mouthed Natasha. If she talked out loud, Rosie Gold would tell on her.

"*Blankets*?" whispered Josie. "What do you mean?"

Just at that moment Miss Heather swished back
into the classroom with a big, bulgy, black plastic
garbage bag. She put it down on the table next to
Josie, and began to untie the string around the
opening of the bag. Rosie Gold pushed forward
to help her. The black bag wobbled on the table
as if there was something alive inside it.

When the string was undone,
color poured out like rain.
Red and gold and orange and
sparkling silver. Midnight
blue and kingfisher blue
and a white as bright as
a field of snow in the
sunlight. There was
forest green and warm

buttery yellow, and a rainbow ball like a patch of oil on the road after rain. The colors met and danced as they rolled out over the table.

"There!" said Miss Heather. "Look what Mr. Stassinopolous has given us for our blanket! Isn't that nice of him? Now, if each of you takes one ball of wool, and knits one square, we can sew them together and make a beautiful warm blanket."

Josie put up her hand. "Miss Heather who is the blanket for?"

"Josie, you weren't listening at all, were you? Now, can someone tell her?"

Rosie Gold's hand wagged in the air, but for once Miss Heather did not choose her. She chose Jason Connolly instead.

"It's a blanket for someone who lives in a city where there's war. For an old person who doesn't have any heating."

"Or a child," chipped in Natasha.

"That's right, Jason," said Miss Heather. "Our blanket is going to go far away to the country I showed you on the map. It will go to help someone keep warm through the hard winter.

A lot of houses and apartments have been damaged by shells because of the war. People are homeless."

"Shells . . ." whispered Josie dreamily, thinking of the glisten of seashells on the sand when the tide went out. "How can shells damage a house?"

"It's not that sort of shell. These shells explode, like bombs. They break walls and windows. They kill people," said Natasha, who always listened when Miss Heather was talking.

"Oh," said Josie. Then she put her hand up.

"Yes, Josie?" said Miss Heather.

"Is it snowing there, where the war is?" asked Josie.

"It snows there all winter long," said Miss Heather, "and often it's too dangerous for people to go out and gather wood to light fires. They get very cold."

11

"Why don't they turn on the heat then?" snickered Darren Fox.

"They don't have central heating there, stupid!" Rosie Gold told him. Miss Heather looked sad.

"Oh yes, they do," she said. "They used to have nice homes with central heating, just like you, before the war. But the bombs and shells have destroyed them. Now, let's give these out. One ball of wool each."

"I should have the gold," said Rosie Gold, "like my name." Everyone wanted the gold, but Rosie got it. A crowd of hands snatched and pulled at the balls of wool. Then, suddenly, they were all gone except for a ball of dark blue that was a bit smaller than the others. Josie

picked it up and squeezed its warm softness.

"It's not fair. Yours is the smallest," said
Natasha.

"I like it," said Josie, and she did.

Miss Heather drew a square on the board

and showed them how many stitches they had
to do. They were allowed to take the wool
home to do their knitting.

"I want this blanket finished by the end
of the week!" said Miss Heather. "Thirty
beautiful squares."

Chapter Two

AT HOME, JOSIE knitted and knitted. Sometimes a hole came in her square and her Mom had to help her pick up the stitches she had dropped. For a long time there was only a little wiggly strip of knitting on her needles, then her square started to grow.

"If I do six more rows tonight, it'll be finished," she told her Mom on Wednesday. Her square looked like a little patch of midnight sky. Josie stroked it and wondered who would get the blanket. Would they like her blue square as much as she did?

That night Josie finished her square. She was not the only one. At school the next morning the tables were covered with finished blanket squares. Red and gold and kingfisher blue, and ebony black, and green as bright as grass in summer. There was white like a snowy field, and a patch like the midnight sky. Miss Heather counted the squares.

"Thirty!" she said happily. "Well done, class. Now, all we have to do is get the squares sewn into a blanket." She looked worried. "But I don't know if I'll have the time to do it. There's a staff meeting this evening."

Josie's hand shot up before anyone else's. "My Mom can do it!" she called out. "She's really good at sewing."

"Are you sure, Josie? Well, that would be a great help. If we fold all the squares and put them back in the bag, will you be able to carry it home?"

"Yes, of course," said Josie.

Her mom looked surprised when Josie tipped the bundle of squares onto the living room carpet. For a moment Josie thought she was going to be angry, but she wasn't.

"But you'll have to help, Josie. I can't do all this on my own," she said.

First, her mom ironed the squares, then they took thin wool and fat needles and started to sew them together. Josie sewed one strip of five squares, and her mom sewed another. Josie

sewed and sewed until her fingers were sore
from pushing the needle through the wool. All
the time she thought about the person in the
cold faraway city who would get the blanket. It
was very late and all the colors of the rainbow
were dancing in front of Josie's eyes.

"Thanks, Josie. You go to bed now. I'll finish
this," her mom said.

When Josie was nearly asleep, Mom brought in the finished blanket. She spread it out on top of Josie's duvet. It was the most beautiful blanket in the world.

"Can I keep it here, just for tonight?" asked Josie.

"Yes, just for tonight," her mom replied.

Josie slept. Her mom went to bed and the sky was as dark as the square of midnight blue Josie had knitted.

Chapter Three

A NOISE LIKE thunder woke Josie up. She sat up
and clutched the blanket. It felt warm and soft
in her fingers, but the room had gone very cold.
Josie shivered and pulled the blanket tight around
her. The thunder rumbled again, and the room
shook. Through the window Josie saw the dark
patch of midnight sky, then a flash like lightning.

"Mom!" she whispered. She was too frightened
to shout.

There was a rustling sound on the other side
of the room, then a voice answered. But it
wasn't her mom's voice. And the room didn't
look like Josie's bedroom any more.

"Hello," the voice said. "Who are you?"

"Josie," whispered Josie.

"Did the shells destroy your apartment? Are you looking for shelter?" asked the voice. It sounded friendly. Josie peered around the room and saw a dark bundle on the floor, against the wall. She wrapped the blanket tight around her and tiptoed across to it. The floor felt like ice under her bare feet.

"You sound scared. You can stay here with me if you want, Josie," said the voice.

Bright flashes like lightning lit the room. Josie saw that the bundle was a girl, curled up to keep warm. She was about the same age as Josie, and she had long dark hair, like Josie's.

Suddenly there was a terrible bang and the floor shook. Josie tripped and fell onto the floor next to the girl.

"That shell came close," said the girl. "I hope it didn't hit any of my friends' homes. Oooh, what's that you've got? It's nice and warm and soft."

"It's a blanket," said Josie. "You can put half of it over you if you want." Josie wriggled close to the girl and spread the blanket over them.

There was another bang and the wall trembled behind Josie's back.

"It's all right," said the girl. "That shell wasn't so close."

"What's your name?" asked Josie.

"Amina."

"Are you all on your own?"

"No," said Amina. "I've got a friend here. Give me your hand." Amina took Josie's hand. "Here, feel," said Amina. Josie felt something soft and warm in Amina's hand. It was even softer than the blanket.

"Pet him," said Amina. "He won't bite you."

The something soft and warm was alive. It wriggled under Josie's fingers. "What is it? A hamster?" asked Josie.

"No, he's my pet mouse. He used to be wild, but I tamed him. He's called Sinta. Only you can't tell, because food is so short and my mom won't let me give him anything to eat."

"Where's your mom?"

"She went out to get wood, before it got dark," said Amina. "Then the shelling started."

As soon as the shells stop, she'll come back. She always does." But Josie felt Amina shivering. How cold and frightened she must be, lying alone on the floor all night, waiting for her mom to come home with wood to start a fire.

"You can have more of the blanket if you want. I'm not cold," said Josie, and she tucked the blanket around Amina.

"Poor little Sinta, I haven't got anything for you tonight," said Amina. "You'll have to wait until Mom gets back."

"What does he eat?" asked Josie.

Amina laughed. "The same as me!" she said. "He hides in my pocket and has a little bit of whatever my mom brings back." There was a soft squeak from Sinta.

"He knows we're talking about food," said Amina. "Where did you get this blanket, Josie? It must be the softest one in the city. It's even warmer than a fire."

"You should see the colors!" said Josie. "It's made of squares of different colors. The one I knitted is dark blue, the same color as the patch of midnight sky in the window."

"I like it when the sky is dark blue, with no shell flashes," said Amina. "That means it's safe. Tell me more about the colors. Everything's so gray and dirty in the city now."

"Well, there's a white square like fluffy snow," began Josie.

"Brrr, don't talk about snow! You'll make me feel cold again!"

"Okay," said Josie, and she tried to think of colors which would make Amina feel warm. "There's yellow and red like the sun when it's setting on a summer evening. There's green like the shade of the trees when we sit under them for a picnic. There's..."

Suddenly the window was full of a blinding white light.

A second later the room rocked. A crash like a thousand storms ripped through the building. It picked up Josie and Amina and threw them across the room. There was a terrible rumbling as if the building was falling apart, and the starlit sky showed where the window had once been. Josie's mouth was full of dust and smoke. She coughed and choked. The blanket was gone, Amina was gone, Sinta was gone. She could smell something burning. How close was it? Was it in the building?

Chapter Four

"AMINA!" JOSIE WHISPERED. She couldn't shout because of all the dust.

"Josie!" came a little croaky voice from under the window.

"What happened? Did something hit us?"

"It was close. The closest so far."

"Is there a fire?"

The light in the window was changing to red. Amina got up and peered out. "There's a fire just down the street," she told Josie. Josie picked herself up off the floor and stumbled

over to Amina. She saw tall red flames
flickering from an apartment building, and
people, like ants, running in the streets. Flames
leapt into the sky, changing it from dark blue to
orange. It was nearly as light as day.

"Poor Sinta," said Amina. "He's so frightened of shells. He's afraid we'll get hit."

"Where is he?"

"In my pocket, right down at the bottom. Can you feel him?" Josie felt the little shivering mouse, deep in Amina's pocket. The walls of Amina's room were shaking too.

"The fire is spreading," said Amina. "It's coming this way. I wish my mom was here."

The fire crackled and rushed. It sounded as if it was nearly in the same room. Then Josie and Amina heard voices shouting. The voices were coming closer and closer.

"Rescuers!" said Amina. "They're coming to get us out!"

The fire was coming closer. Which would get to them first, the fire or the rescuers? Josie grabbed Amina's hand and they stumbled to the broken doorway. There was so much smoke that their eyes hurt. Josie coughed when she tried to breathe, and the fire roared like a lion outside. Suddenly the girls could hear the rescuers' voices on the other side of the door.

"We're in here!" shouted Amina.

Chapter Five

THE DOOR FLEW open. Josie blinked as the bright sun streamed across her bed. Her mom was pulling back the curtains.

"Come on, Josie, you'll be late for school," said her mom, "and you've got to take that blanket in, remember."

Josie felt on the bed for the blanket. It was there, as bright and beautiful as ever, all the colors of the rainbow.

"Amina!" whispered Josie. Where was Amina?

Josie picked up the blanket. It smelled of smoke and danger. It smelled of war. Where was Amina now?

Miss Heather packed the blanket up in a parcel and sent it away. Weeks passed. Everybody had forgotten about the blanket, except Josie. Then one day Miss Heather came into the classroom waving a big brown envelope.

"Class!" she said. "We have a letter about our blanket. And some photographs."

Miss Heather rustled through the envelope and held up a big photograph.

"Look," she said. "These are the people who have lost their homes because of the war. Their houses were shelled, and now they're in a center for homeless people. If you look carefully, you can see the blankets on their beds. One of them is the blanket we made."

The photograph showed a crowd of people huddled together in a big hall. There was a row of beds with blankets on them. And by one of the beds, there was a girl, about Josie's age, with long dark hair. Josie stared. Surely she knew that face. Josie could not stay in her chair. She had to get closer to the photograph.

"Josie!" said Miss Heather. But Josie was staring at the face of the dark-haired girl.

"Amina!" she whispered. "It's Amina! The girl in my dream!"

It *was* Amina in the photograph. And one hand was in her pocket. Josie knew she was petting Sinta.

"Sit down, Josie!" said Miss Heather crossly, and Josie had to sit down.

"Our blanket is on one of those beds," said Miss Heather.

But Josie knew it was on Amina's bed. *Amina isn't a dream*, she thought, *she's a real girl. My dream was real. Amina had to leave her home because of the shelling and the fire.*

The blanket was on Amina's bed in the center for homeless people. All the colors of the rainbow were there. The red, the gold, the orange, the forest green, the snowy white, and the midnight blue that Josie had knitted. The blanket would wrap around Amina at night and keep her warm.

"Sleep well, Amina," said Josie, so softly that no one heard her.

YELLOW BANANAS

Don't forget there's a whole bunch of Yellow Bananas to choose from: